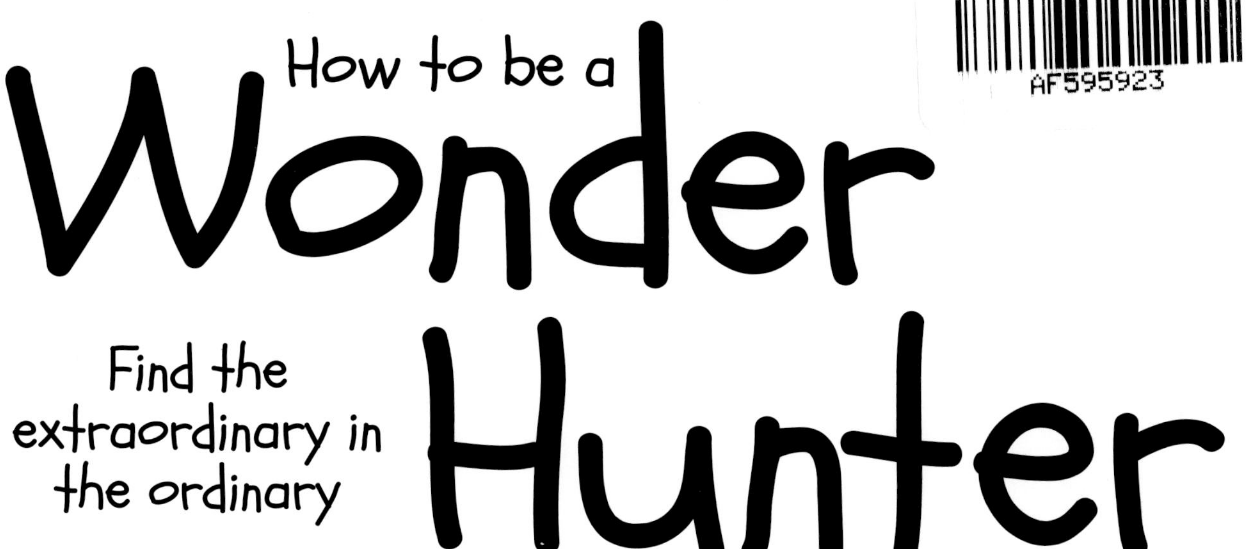
How to be a
Wonder
Hunter
Find the extraordinary in the ordinary

Big Sky Publishing Pty Ltd
PO Box 303, Newport, NSW 2106, Australia
Phone: 1300 364 611
Fax: (61 2) 9918 2396
Email: info@bigskypublishing.com.au
Web: www.bigskypublishing.com.au

Cover design: Think Productions
Typesetting: Think Productions
Printed by KS Printing

A catalogue record for this book is available from the National Library of Australia

How to be a Wonder Hunter

Find the extraordinary in the ordinary

BIG SKY PUBLISHING
www.bigskypublishing.com.au

written and illustrated by Josh Langley

For Sue.

Life doesn't have to just be about schoolwork, watching TV and picking up dog poo.

It can be way cooler than computer games, chatting online and watching funny videos.

Life is totally next level when you become a

WONDER HUNTER!

Live the Wonder

Hunter Life

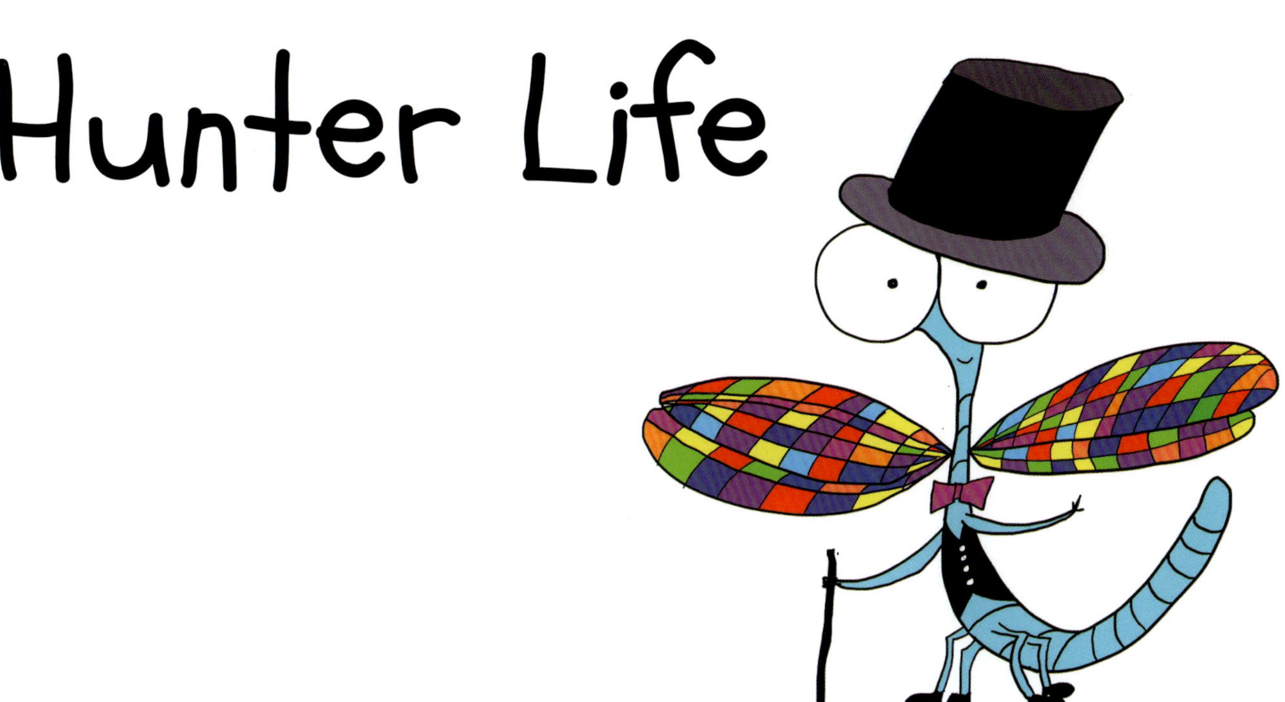

Being a Wonder Hunter makes everything way more playful and much more fun than you could ever imagine.

You get to go on exciting journeys, explore new places, discover weird and wonderful things and create all kinds of ideas and stories.

Are you ready to become a Wonder Hunter?

The Wonder

Hunter Toolkit

You already have everything you need to be a Wonder Hunter.

A BODY

Your size, shape or ability doesn't matter.
Anyone can be a Wonder Hunter.

Yes, anyone.

SENSES

You'll need all or some of the following ...

... eyes, ears, nose, tongue and skin (good for holding your guts in).

You use these senses to feel and notice the world around you.

AN IMAGINATION

Your brain already comes preloaded with an imagination.

That's where your ideas come from.

A CURIOUS MIND

Have you ever asked a question?

Then you have a curious mind.

DREAMS

We all dream at night, and it's good to remember what we dream about.

It's a different way our minds can make sense of things and solve problems.

Training to be Wonder Hunter

Step 1: Learn to notice stuff.

When you start to notice what's around you,
it's amazing what you can discover.

It's like finding treasure!

What can you notice around you right now?

What can you really see?

you are
loved
you're a wonder
hunter
tortellini
spaghetti
you are amazing

Now listen.

What sounds can you hear?

What can you smell?

Start noticing in different places.
Your bedroom, the backyard, at school,
or by a small creek.

If you want to see what it's like to really see something, try watching a ladybird through a magnifying glass.

Discover new places by finding out where the ants are going.

Notice what rain smells like.

Training to be a Wonder Hunter

Step 2:
Find the wonder of food.

Food is a doorway to new and exciting experiences.

So, open up and let the flavours in.

What new foods can you try?

Pick a country and discover its National dish.

Or make up something new.
How about putting spaghetti
in an ice cream cone?

Yum

Training to be a Wonder Hunter

Step 3:
Enjoy the wonder of daydreaming.

As a Wonder Hunter your imagination is one of the most powerful things you have.

You can take your imagination
with you everywhere.

To the toilet, to the shops, to school.

With your imagination, you can:

go on adventures,

create stories,

make new worlds,

and imagine doing things you never thought you could.

Use your imagination to help overcome fears, solve problems or to practise for something in real life.

Reading lots of different books will fire your imagination and take you on lots of adventures.

You're going on an adventure right now just by reading this book!

Wonder Hunter
words and illustrations by Josh Langley

Training to be a Wonder Hunter

Step 4:
Ask the wonder questions.

A Wonder Hunter should always be wondering about something – it keeps the wonder alive!

‘I wonder what makes me angry?’

‘I wonder what makes me happy?’

'I wonder why I think the thoughts I do?'

‘I wonder if birds are ever afraid of heights?’

'I wonder what it's like to be someone else?'

'I wonder what my dreams mean?'

'Where do they come from?'

The Wonder Hunter

Final Checklist

✓ Body

✓ Senses

✓ Imagination

✓ Curious mind

✓ Notice new things around you

✓ Try different foods

✓ Explore your imagination

✓ Be curious about life

✓ Ask lots of questions

✓ Read lots of books

✓ Remember your dreams

CONGRATULATIONS!

You are now officially a Wonder Hunter!

Life will never be boring again.

Here's your Wonder Hunter ID badge.

Job Title: Wonder Hunter.

Job Description: Find the wonder in life.

WH
WONDER HUNTER
JOSH

Time to go Wonder Hunting!

But before you do, let me share a story...

When I was a kid, I found a very old notebook in the back of the garden shed. It was hidden behind a pile of wood. On the cover it said, 'Wonder Hunting – a field guide'. Then on the inside page, there was a message that read:

To Josh, keep this book close as it holds the secret to living a wonder-full life.

Yours forever,

Josh from 2022.

I wonder...

Thank you to the wonder-full team at Big Sky Publishing for believing in this magical little book: Diane, Sharon, Allison, Jodee and Denny.

Thank you to Andy for believing in me.

Thank you to you for reading this book.

I think you're wonder-full!

You can now watch Josh talk about the themes of his books with the Inspiring Kids video series.

www.joshlangley.com.au

Module 1 - Self-Awareness & Self-Acceptance

Even cool kids have to poo!

It's Ok to be different!

No-one is perfect!

Every 'body' is just fine

Being You is Enough

Noticing your thoughts

PARENTS START HERE:

Download Parent Guide

Download Activity Sheets

Download Affirmation Posters

Talk nicely to our body

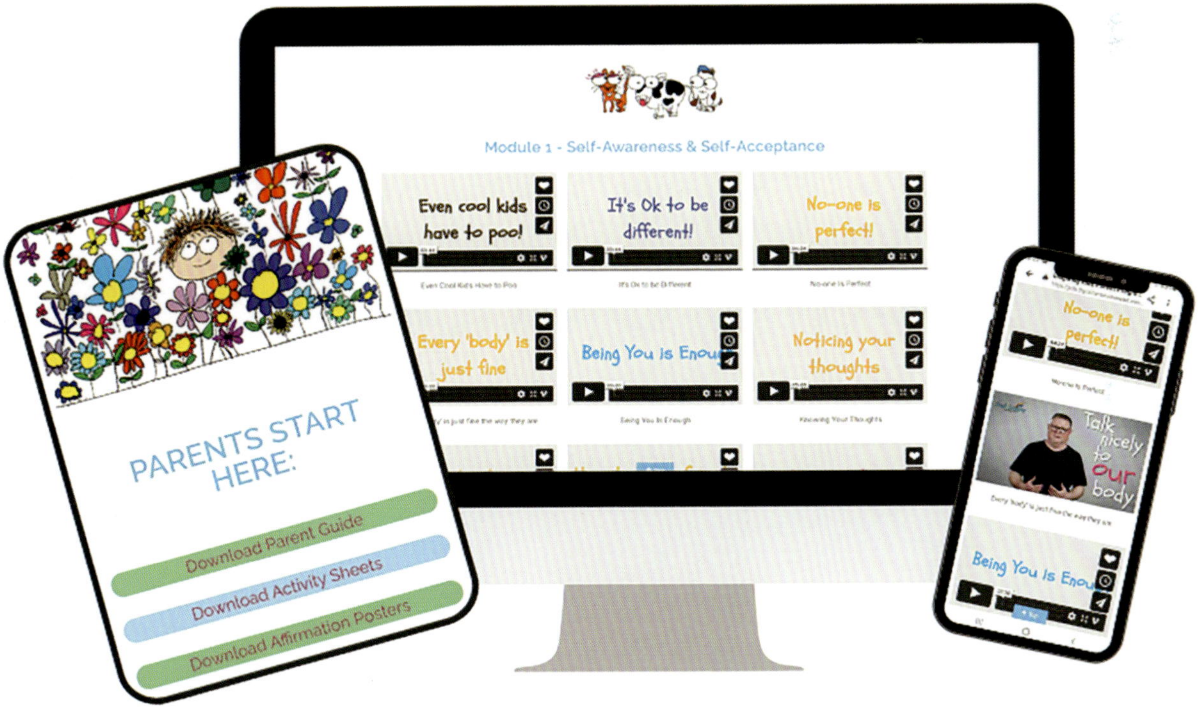

www.joshlangley.com.au

Other books in the
Being You is Enough series

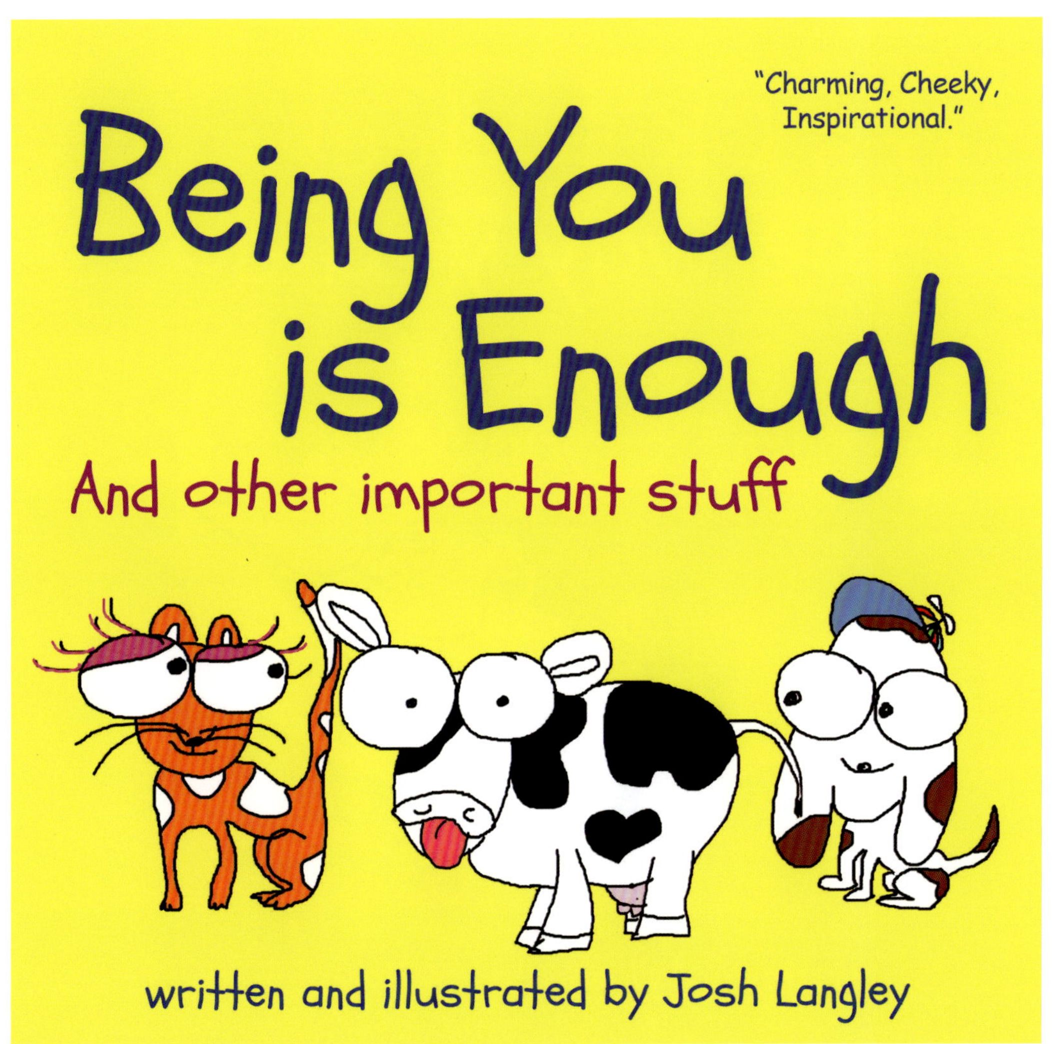
"Charming, Cheeky, Inspirational."
Being You is Enough
And other important stuff
written and illustrated by Josh Langley

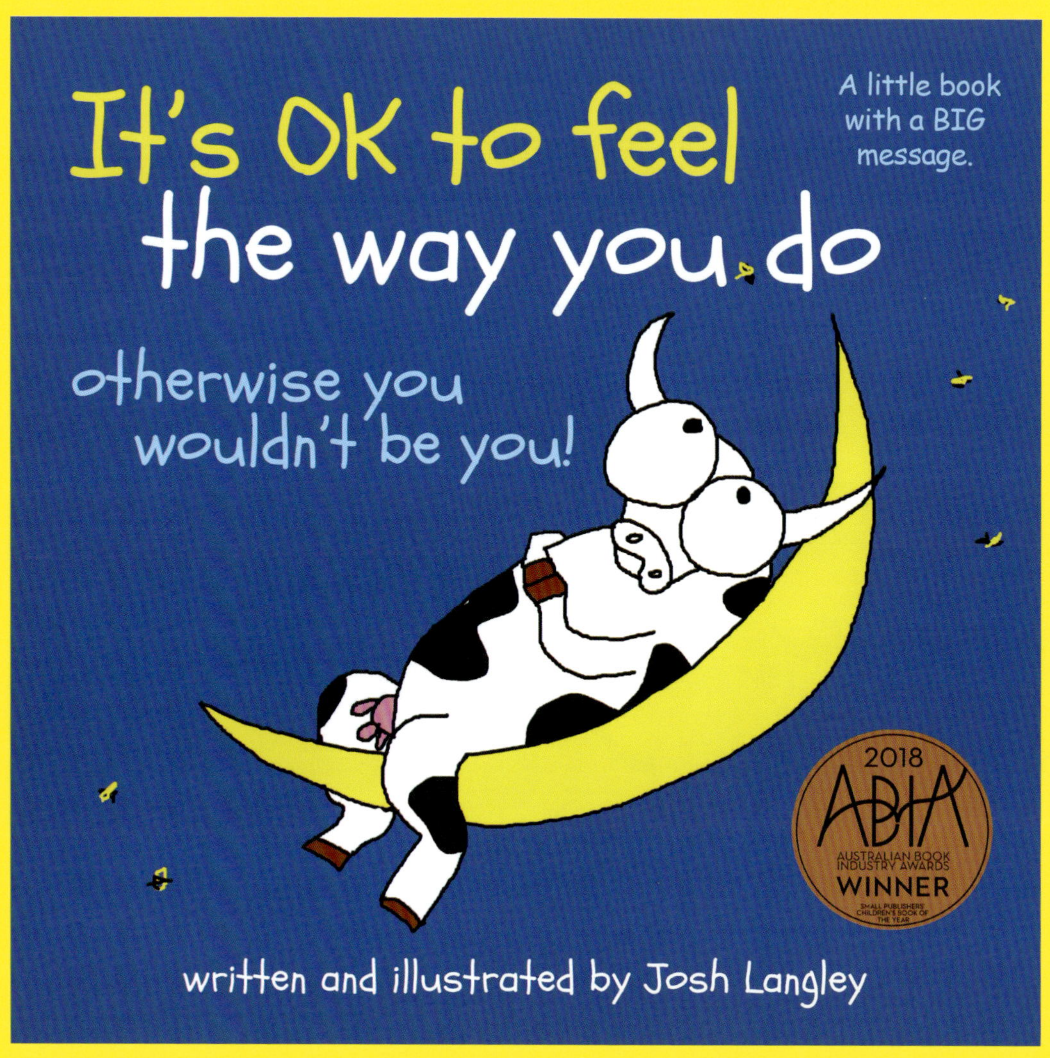
It's OK to feel the way you do
A little book with a BIG message.
otherwise you wouldn't be you!
2018
ABIA
AUSTRALIAN BOOK INDUSTRY AWARDS
WINNER
SMALL PUBLISHERS CHILDREN'S BOOK OF THE YEAR
written and illustrated by Josh Langley

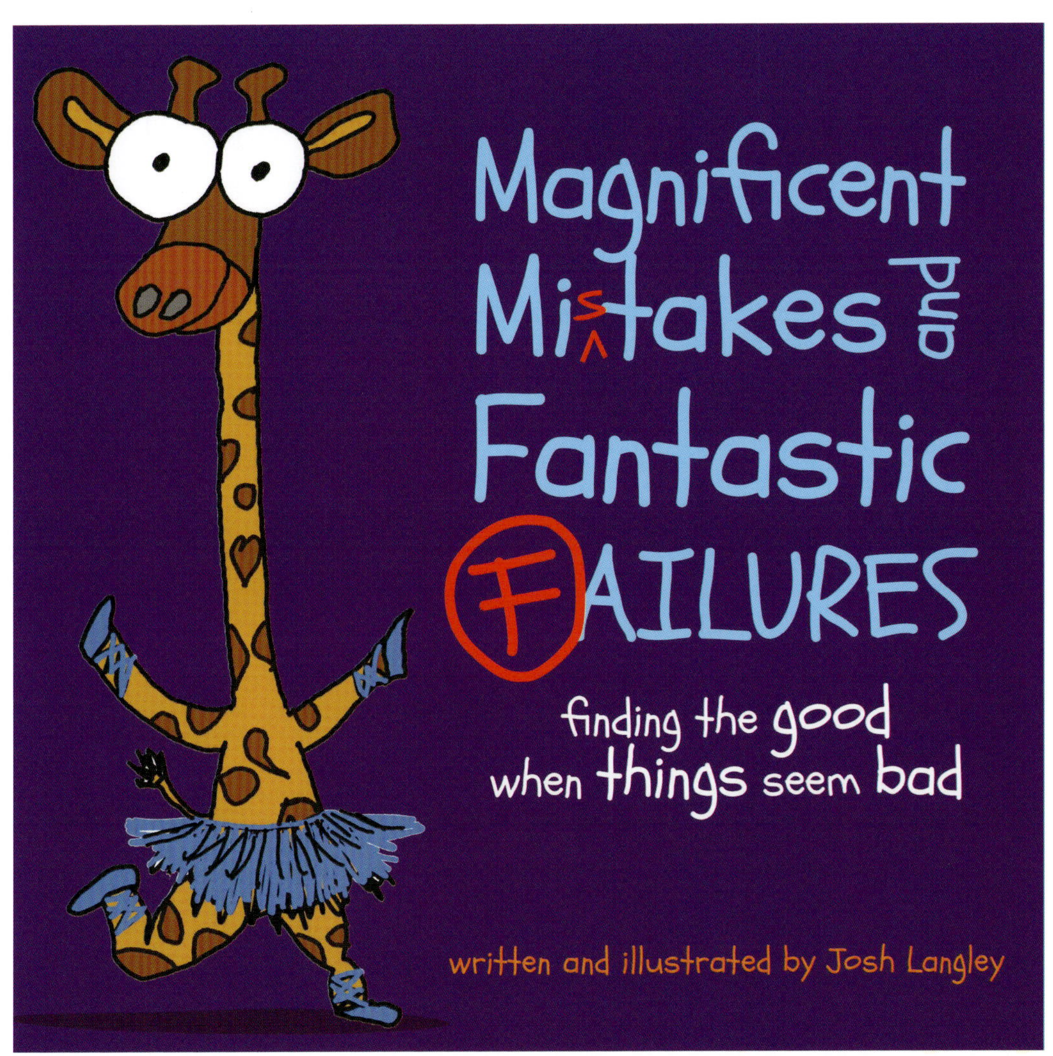
Magnificent
Mistakes and
Fantastic
FAILURES
finding the good
when things seem bad
written and illustrated by Josh Langley

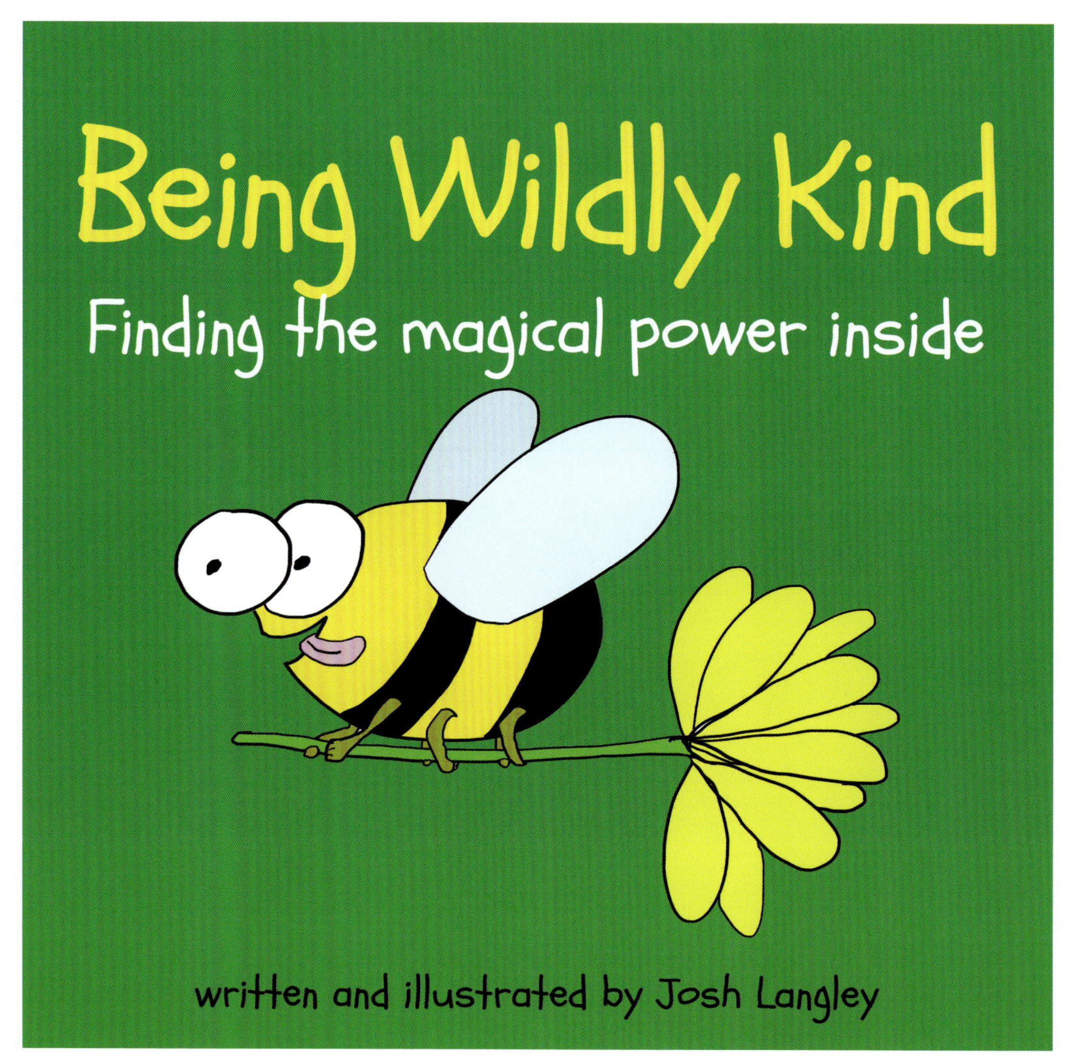
Being Wildly Kind
Finding the magical power inside
written and illustrated by Josh Langley

frog and the **well**

unconventional happiness

Celebrating the absurd and wonderful

Illustrations and words by josh langley

follow your heart

everyday wisdom for an extraordinary life

Illustrations and words by josh langley

For more great books by Josh
and other authors visit

www.bigskypublishing.com.au